D0604869

A Home Named
WALTER

Chelsea Lin Wallace

Illustrated by Ginnie Hsu

Feiwel and Friends
New York

Walter was once a home.

He treasured the noise. He relished the mess. He liked the hustle and bustle.

But what he loved most was the warmth of family.

Then one day . . . they moved out.

Walter's feelings were hurt.

He let his grass turn brown and his plumbing rust.

He let his floors creak and his doors droop.

And there he sat.

A cold, quiet, empty house,
growing weeds all around.

(And he liked it that way.)

Then one day, a family burst
through his ragged doors.

"This is our new house?"
asked Little Girl.

Mama carried boxes.
Little Girl carried a picture.

"It's cozy,"
said Mama.

Walter felt cramped.

"It feels different," said Little Girl.

Walter felt different, too.

"It will feel better once we unpack," said Mama.

Walter wasn't sure that would help him feel better at all.

He knew there was only one thing to do . . .

Get. Them. Out.

"Let's open the shutters," said Mama.

Walter slammed them shut.

"Let's bake cookies," said Little Girl.

He refused to bake.

"We could make a fire in the fireplace."

But he quickly snuffed out the flame.

"This house seems to have some personality," said Mama.

"He will fit right in with us," said Little Girl.

Mama and Little Girl
fixed all the quirks
in the house.

But Walter didn't want to be fixed.
He wanted to be left alone!

Walter was just about to
rattle his pipes when he heard
a sniffle.

Little Girl was sitting on the
bed looking at her picture.

"I miss you, Papa.
You'd like our new house.
He's funny, like you."

Walter felt something coursing through his walls he hadn't felt in a long time.

He tried to hold it back . . .

But suddenly, his pipes burst!

His tears dripped into every room.

Mama scrambled for buckets and pails.

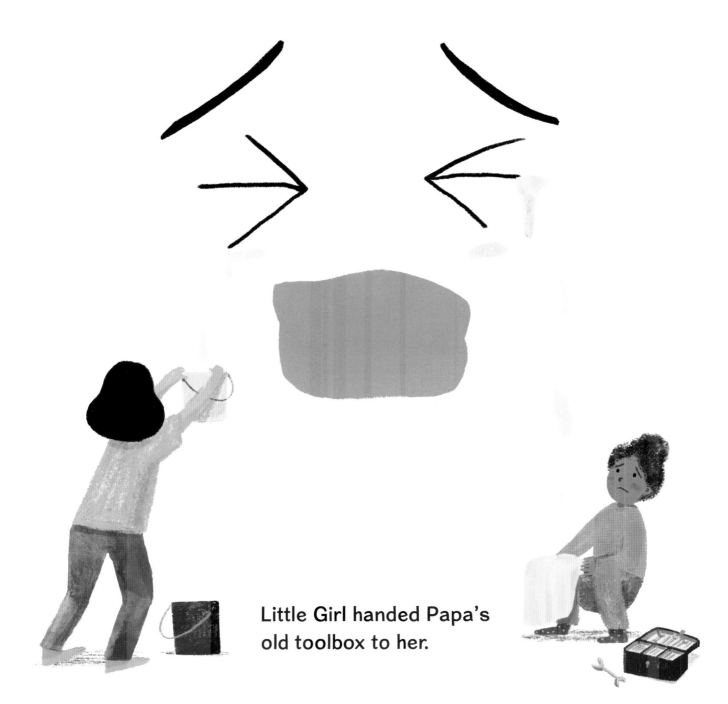

Little Girl handed Papa's
old toolbox to her.

And she asked,
"Why is our house crying?"

Mama said, "It's just a leak, dear.
Will you grab me some towels?"

Little Girl went looking.

She opened a drawer in the hallway and found an old photograph.

She saw a very different Walter with a family standing in front of him.

That's when she realized.

"I'm sorry you are sad, House.
I know what it's like to have
someone move away.

But it doesn't mean you're alone."

Walter's tears stopped.

He felt warm. He felt understood.
But most of all, he felt . . . livable.

Walter watched as Mama
sang to Little Girl.
Walter watched them
snuggle as two.

He smelled the fire in his fireplace . . .
and tasted the cookies in his oven.

"Now say good night to everyone and go to bed."

"Good night, Mama.
Good night, Papa."

And as she fell asleep . . .

"Good night, House."

His once quiet hallways echoed with laughter.

His once closed shutters let in the breeze.

His once empty rooms filled with family.

And all at once . . .

he felt like a *home*.

(And he liked it that way.)

For Mom and Dad who made every house
feel like home, and for Charlee and Michael who
make home feel like love. —C.L.W.

To mom, thank you for bringing me to the world. —G.H.

A Feiwel and Friends Book
An imprint of Macmillan Publishing Group, LLC
120 Broadway, New York, NY 10271
mackids.com

Our books may be purchased in bulk for promotional, educational, or business use.
Please contact your local bookseller or the Macmillan Corporate and Premium Sales Department at
(800) 221-7945 ext. 5442 or by email at MacmillanSpecialMarkets@macmillan.com.

Library of Congress Cataloging-in-Publication Data is available

First edition, 2022

Book design by Mike Burroughs
The illustrations were created using acrylic gouache, colored pencils, and Photoshop.
Feiwel and Friends logo designed by Filomena Tuosto
Printed in China by RR Donnelley Asia Printing Solutions Ltd., Dongguan City, Guangdong Province

ISBN 978-1-250-31641-7 (hardcover)
1 3 5 7 9 10 8 6 4 2